For my mum, Margaret. Thanks for what you did.
SH

For my mother, Isobel.
BL

First published in 2009
by Walker Books Australia Pty Ltd
Locked Bag 22, Newtown
NSW 2042 Australia
www.walkerbooks.com.au

The moral rights of the author and illustrator have been asserted.

National Library of Australia Cataloguing-in-Publication entry:

Holt, Sharon.
Your mother didn't do that! / Sharon Holt; illustrator Brian Lovelock.

1st ed.
ISBN: 978 1 921150 17 3 (hbk.)

Mother and child – Juvenile fiction.
Other Authors/Contributors: Lovelock, Brian, 1956-

NZ823.3

The illustrations for this book are mixed media, comprising watercolour, acrylic ink and coloured pencil
Typeset in Village
Printed and bound in China

2 4 6 8 10 9 7 5 3 1

Your Mother Didn't Do That!

SHARON HOLT &
BRIAN LOVELOCK

WALKER BOOKS
AND SUBSIDIARIES

LONDON • BOSTON • SYDNEY • AUCKLAND

Holly didn't want Mum to go out.

"Dad will tell you a story,"
said Mum.

"Yes," said Dad. "I'll tell you about
the night you were born."

"Okay," said Holly.
"Did I hatch out of an egg
like a chicken?"

"No," said Dad. "If you were a
new chick, your mother would
have fluffed up her feathers and
sat on you to keep you safe.
Your mother didn't do that."

Holly laughed.

"What if I was a kitten?"

"If you were a kitten, your mother
would have licked you all over,"
said Dad. "Your mother didn't do that."

Holly giggled as Dad licked the air with his tongue.

"What about a baby kangaroo?"

"If you were a baby kangaroo,
your mother would have kept you
in her pocket," said Dad. He looked
in his pocket and shook his head.
"Your mother didn't do that."

"What if I was a baby owl?"
asked Holly.

"If you were a baby owl, your mother would have fed you mice," said Dad. "Your mother didn't do that."

Holly and Dad pulled faces at the thought of eating mice.

"What if I was a baby shark?"

"You don't want to hear about
baby sharks," said Dad.

"Yes, I do," said Holly. "What would
my mother do if I was a baby shark?"

"Well," said Dad. "When a
mother shark gives birth, she has
so many baby sharks that she
eats some of them for dinner!"

Holly hid under the blankets.

"Don't worry," said Dad.
"Your mother would never do that."

"Good," said Holly.
"I'm glad my mother wasn't a shark.
What if I was a baby seahorse?"

"If you were a baby seahorse, your father would have looked after you in his belly," said Dad.

"Really?" said Holly. "Did you look after me in your belly?"

"No," said Dad. "Mums are much better at that. Mum looked after you and I looked after Mum."

"So what did Mum do when I was a new baby?" asked Holly.

"When you were a new baby,
your mother held you close to her
heart and cried and cried," said Dad.

Holly looked worried.
"Was she very sad?" she asked.

"No," said Dad, tucking Holly in to bed.
"They were happy tears. When you were
born, your mother was the happiest mum
in the world. And I was the happiest dad
in the world."

Holly smiled.

"And I was the happiest
baby in the world."